TONY HAWK'S
900 revolution

VOLUME 11

Tony Hawk's 900 Revolution
is published by Stone Arch Books
a Capstone imprint, 1710 Roe Crest Drive, North Mankato,
MN 56003 www.capstonepub.com Copyright © 2013
by Stone Arch Books. All rights reserved. No part of this
publication may be reproduced in whole or in part, or stored
in a retrieval system, or transmitted in any form or by any
means, electronic, mechanical, photocopying, recording, or
otherwise, without written permission of the publisher.

Cataloging-in-Publication Data is available on the Library
of Congress website.
ISBN: 978-1-4342-3842-9 (library binding)
ISBN: 978-1-4342-4895-4 (paperback)

Summary: The Collective, in possession of the Fragmented
board and growing stronger every day, decides to
retrieve one of their own: Tommy Goff, held captive by
the Revolution in an undisclosed location. To discover
the prisoner's whereabouts, Elliot Addison and his mentor
Archard Venin must earn the Revolution's trust. But Archard
has other plans—the destruction of the Revolution, and the
death of his old friend, Eldrick Otus.

Photo and Vector Graphics Credits: Shutterstock.
Photo credit page 122, Bart Jones/ Tony Hawk,

Cover Illustrator: Wilson Toltosa
Cover Colorist: Benny Fuentes
Graphic Designer: Kay Fraser

Printed in China.
092012
006936RRDS13

FLIPSIDE

BY BRANDON TERRELL // ILLUSTRATED BY CAIO MAJADO

VOLUME 11

STONE ARCH BOOKS
a capstone imprint

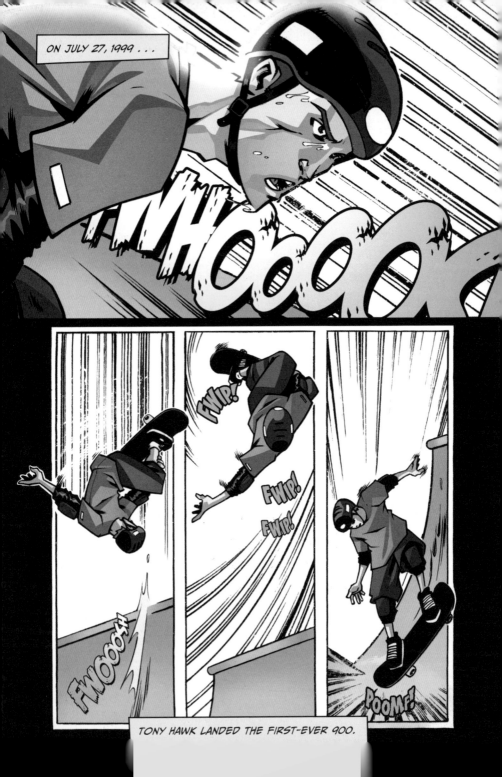

1

As he opened his eyes and struggled to regain consciousness, sixteen-year-old Mikey Singer realized he couldn't see a thing. Panic raced through him as he felt the fabric of a black wool cap over his head. The stocking cap had been pulled past his eyes and down to his chin. When he exhaled, his warm breath absorbed into the woven fabric, nearly stifling him with its heat.

Where am I? He felt like Rip Van Winkle waking from twenty years of slumber. His memory was sluggish. He recalled bits and pieces: being chased by teenagers on skateboards, huddling in a New York alley behind a dumpster ripe with rotting garbage, the sting of a dart piercing his neck, and the wave of unconsciousness that washed over him.

Now, he was slumped on a sofa somewhere, his hands tied uncomfortably behind him. The back of his neck itched, but he could not reach it. He tried to move his legs, but they were still heavy with sleep. Pinpricks of tingling pain coursed through them.

A door opened, and he heard footsteps. Two sets. A voice said, "Up and at 'em, Sleeping Beauty," and then hands clasped around his biceps. He was hauled to his feet. When it was clear he could not stand on his own, his two captors unwound the binding on his wrists and slung his arms over their shoulders. As one, the three began to walk. The toes of Mikey's skate shoes dragged along the floor as they moved.

"Geez, Rodney, how much did you tranq him?" questioned one of the captors.

"The usual," responded the other. "Probably hit him harder because the dude's scrawny as a toothpick."

It was true. Mikey was rail thin. He'd spent months hiding out in New York, crashing on friends' futons or in their cars or sometimes even on the streets. His meals consisted of vending machine snacks or food stolen from convenience stores. He didn't want to go back to Benny and Jeannine, his foster parents. Because of him, they'd suffered terrible beatings.

Because of him, his foster brother Slider was missing. Mikey had been hiding from something—and someone—he didn't understand. In fact, Mikey still carried with him the scars from his first encounter with the shadowy group, in the form of a light crease from his bottom lip to his chin. All because of a cigar box containing the broken tail of a skateboard, something called a Fragment. He had no clue why the stupid thing was important, just that it was.

A door opened, and the two teens awkwardly carried him through. Classical music softly filtered through the room. Mikey was shoved down into a wooden rail back chair. The wool cap was roughly yanked off his head, and he could see again.

He was in a luxurious office blanketed with shadows. It was night outside, and the only light in the room spilled from a lamp resting on a long, wooden desk. Behind the desk were numerous shelves, all of them crammed full of books. An antique record player proved to be the source of the lilting music.

A man stood with his back to Mikey. He was looking out a large window. Mikey could see the glittering lights of a city, along with—*Holy crap, is that the Eiffel Tower?*

"Welcome to Paris, Michael," the man said, confirming Mikey's unasked question. The man's voice had a trace of a French accent. "My apologies for the rather crude travel arrangements."

There was a snicker to Mikey's left. He turned and saw the two teens who'd carried him to the room. Anger flushed through him as he recognized the hulking kid with a buzz-cut and his partner in crime, the scowling teen who had left his mark on Mikey's lip.

"Buzzer? Rodney? You're free to go." The man dismissed the hoods with a wave. Grumbling under their breaths, the duo exited.

"What do you want?" said Mikey.

The man, middle-aged with salt-and-pepper hair and a chiseled face like carved stone, walked over and leaned against the desk. "My name is Archard Venin. And the question isn't what I want. It's who I want."

Venin wheeled a cart of fresh cooked steak, vegetables, and bread in front of Mikey. "Please, Michael, eat up," he said.

Mikey eagerly devoured the food, cramming his mouth with bread until he was practically choking on it.

"Let me ask you, Michael," Venin said, "are you by chance a chess player?"

Mikey looked over a forkful of steak and flashed a look that said, *Seriously?*

"Didn't think so." Venin smiled. "You see, I'm engaged in a very important game of chess right now with a man named Eldrick Otus, the leader of a group of teenage thrill-seekers known as the Revolution. I've spent a long time setting up this particular game, years of strategically placing my pieces on the board. And there's a young man named Thomas Goff, who happens to be one of my most important pieces. A rook, for sure.

"Michael, Eldrick Otus has taken my rook off the board. And the...organization...I work for would like your help getting him back."

Mikey swallowed. He could feel his energy returning. His mind was clear and focused now, like he was standing with the nose of his deck over the coping of a half-pipe, ready to drop in.

"Look," Mikey said, "my brother's missing because of you guys. Why would I help you?"

Venin ignored Mikey's question. "Your brother is not missing. He is a member of the Revolution."

"He's what?" asked Mikey, shocked.

"Slider has been working for Eldrick Otus," added Venin.

Mikey felt the pressure around his heart unraveling. After all the months of transient living, concerned for Slider's safety above all else, knowing that his brother was all right made him feel like the world wasn't tilted off its axis anymore.

"What I need is really quite simple, Michael," Venin continued. "On a computer within Otus's facility is the location of where he's imprisoned Thomas. All you have to do is access it for me."

"And you want me to use Slider to get into this... facility?" asked Mikey.

"Precisely."

"No dice," said the young man.

Mikey's unquestioned stance clearly aggravated the old man. Venin silently made his way back to the window. The city's lights sparkled across the glass, reflected in his eyes and on his stony features. Finally, he said, "Michael, will you please touch the back of your neck?"

Mikey slowly reached back and explored the nape of his neck. There, he found a small incision, barely an inch in length. Something was under the skin, something hard. Mikey delicately scratched at it.

"What did you do to me?" he asked.

"I've implanted a device that monitors both your location and your audio." Venin reached into his suit coat's interior breast pocket and removed a slender electronic component. "It is also capable of delivering an electronic pulse to your brain. One zap, and your memory is an empty hard drive. Every skateboarding trick, every girl you ever kissed, all of those precious moments you and Slider spent together? Forgotten. Forever. Do I have your attention now?"

Goosebumps pricked up along Mikey's arms. This was insane. Suddenly, all he wanted to do was claw at his neck, remove the device with his own fingers.

"I'll ask you again," said Venin. "Michael, will you help me?"

The record player had reached its end, filling the room with the static, rhythmical sound of its needle bumping against the turntable.

Finally, Mikey nodded.

Venin smiled. "Good answer. Oh, one more thing."

Mikey looked up with hesitant, uncertain eyes.

Venin's face broke into a wide grin. "What shall we have for dessert?"

2

Tommy Goff had the same routine every morning: wake up, exercise, shower, eat whatever breakfast the guys upstairs brought down for him, watch TV, and wait for the Collective to rescue him.

He'd been sequestered for months now in what could best be described as a modified bomb shelter. It wasn't like a typical cement bunker, though. It had a living room, a bathroom, a small bedroom, and an exercise area. It was kind of like being grounded in someone else's house.

Despite the "normal" arrangements, Tommy was itching to be free again. It'd been forever since he'd been on a skateboard.

Tommy felt the liberating rush of cruising down places like Seacoast Drive, popping off nollies and kickflips with ease. He could practically feel the absence left in his mind and spirit since his Fragment, a piece of Tony Hawk's legendary 900 board, had been taken from him in Hawaii by his best friend, Omar Grebes, and his ridiculous Revolution.

This morning's breakfast was oatmeal and an English muffin. As Tommy snatched up the plate left just inside the bunker's main entrance—a cement door with a small, sliding metal door near its base—he could vaguely hear the sound of voices upstairs. He'd never seen the men Otus had hired to watch him, but by listening closely, he could tell there were no more than four guards at one time.

Tommy abandoned the plate on the coffee table. He wasn't hungry this morning. He decided to break from his routine, to crank the treadmill on high, and to run as fast as he could.

He straddled the machine's conveyor belt and plugged the earbuds of his MP3 player in his ears. When the tread was blazing at high speed, and his tunes were cranked to a near deafening level, Tommy leaped on and sprinted at full speed.

Within minutes, his lungs burned and his legs ached. But he kept a fast pace, closing his eyes and imagining that he was running along the beach, under the Imperial Beach Pier. He was a kid again....

***

Years earlier, Tommy cranked the dial on his boombox, laid back on his bed, and let punk music rattle the framed posters and photos on his bedroom walls. His mom would come by any second and tell him to turn it down. Until then, he was going to absorb the music, let it move him like an earthquake.

Sure enough, on cue, a hand pounded loudly on his door. "Thomas! Turn that music down! Now!"

"Sure, Ma!" He thumbed the dial down just enough to get her off his back.

"You have company!" she added.

Tommy swung his legs off the bed, rushed to the door, and opened it. Standing there was Omar.

"What up?" eleven-year-old Tommy asked. Then he and his nine-year old best bud engaged in the most elaborate secret handshake ever conceived.

"Check it!" Omar said, holding a new skateboard in his left hand. It was blue with a bright yellow decal of an owl on the bottom and sick-looking yellow wheels.

"Gnarly, bro!" Tommy snatched the board from Omar's hands. He carried it over to his bed and plopped down to examine it. Omar went right for the assorted VHS tapes Tommy had lined up beneath his 13-inch television set. Hooked to the TV via a mess of colorful cables was a VHS camcorder, one of his dad's old relics that miraculously still worked.

Tommy spun the composite wheels, ran his fingers over the rough grip tape on the board's nose. "You ready to test this bad boy out?" he asked.

Omar waved a videotape in the air. "Not without a little inspiration."

The video was a compilation of some of the sweetest skateboarding tricks the boys had ever seen. They watched as all-stars like Bucky Lasek performed the near-impossible forward to fakie Indy 720, landing on the vert ramp backward. They marveled as Nyjah Huston nailed a perfect nollie heel back lip down a huge rail—and of course, Tom Schaar's first 1080. With each clip, the boys cheered like they were watching the maneuvers live.

The best trick was saved for last, though. When the logo for the 1999 X-Games flashed on screen, Tommy's excitement skyrocketed.

"Here it is!" Tommy said. He smacked Omar on the shoulder, as if getting his attention was necessary.

"The day I was born," Omar whispered. It was true. The day captured by the worn VHS tape was the same day Zeke and Rachel Grebes were welcoming their son into the world.

Tommy sat on the edge of his bed as Tony Hawk raced down the half-pipe, gained speed, and shot up the other side. In midair, he performed a magnificent 900, the greatest accomplishment in skateboarding history. After completing the move, the Birdman stood atop the platform, holding his deck in the air in triumph. The crowd roared. The announcers were flabbergasted by the stunning vertical display.

Just then, as it always did, the tape briefly glitched. The image jumped and shifted, flaring white before righting itself again. Tommy clicked the remote, freezing the frame on Hawk's wide smile.

"Come on," he told Omar. "Let's go shred some sidewalks."

The boys strapped on helmets and pads, and carved their way through the neighborhood. They stopped at Mar Vista High School, skating their way through the school's outdoor concrete courtyard.

Tommy, a daredevil on his deck, ollied up and locked his trucks in a backside 50/50 grind along a dual metal staircase railing. Omar looked fluid on his new board, popping a textbook heelflip off a curb behind the school despite only recently learning the trick from his dad.

Because of their fathers' friendship, the two boys had known each other since they were toddlers. And it showed in the way they skated. It was like they could anticipate each other's moves, were inside each other's heads and riding the same brainwave. Without a word, they wove between one another, narrowly avoiding a collision but never scared it would happen, before pulling off side-by-side manuals along the school's outdoor basketball court.

They rode like this for hours, trying to outdo one another with killer moves until the streetlights came on, signifying the end of another picture-perfect California day.

A few hours later, Tommy's peeked into his son's bedroom. "Lights out, Chief," he said.

"Yeah," Tommy replied, his nose deep in a skateboarding magazine.

"I mean it," his dad said with a chuckle, flicking off the light switch.

The bedroom plunged into darkness and left Tommy unable to see the article he was reading.

"Hey!" Tommy jokingly yelled.

"Goodnight, kiddo," said his dad.

"Night, Pops."

Moonlight filtered through the tree branches outside his window, casting irregular shadows on his wall and highlighting the broken skateboards, surfing posters, and photos plastered on it.

Tommy could not sleep. For nearly an hour, he stared at the images, imagining a future where he and Omar were world-famous skateboarders with sponsors and endorsement deals, traveling the globe, meeting girls and impressing them with their unique half-pipe and street tricks.

Into his hazy, half-awake dreams and aspirations came the sound of his parents arguing.

Again.

Tommy rolled over and pressed the pillow against his ear, hoping to shut out the noise. But he could still hear their muffled voices.

"…don't care, Henry!"

"But I have to, Irene…wish you'd understand…"

"…he told you to jump, you'd ask how high…"

"…I've sacrificed so much so Tommy could fulfill…"

"…leave our son out of this! He won't become…"

Tommy slithered under the covers, smothering himself with the pillow, using it to dry his eyes.

A short time later, the door to his room creaked open. He stirred, caught in the space between awake and dreaming. He could see the silhouette of his father framed in the doorway. He wasn't sure why, but Tommy kept his eyes closed and pretended to be asleep.

His father came over and sat on the edge of the bed. The extra weight was familiar and comfortable. Tommy recalled the years when his father would snuggle up beside him and read him fairy tales or tell him stories of magical creatures and heroic journeys.

Tommy heard a sniffle and realized that his father was crying. He had never heard the stoic man cry before. It was alarming, a sign that the world was about to change.

Without a word, Henry Goff placed his hand atop Tommy's head, stood, and walked out the door.

He never saw his father again…

***

…Tommy stabbed angrily at the treadmill, killing the power.

The whirring belt slowed to a crawl, and Tommy's breakneck pace slowed with it. There was a hitch in his side, and every muscle in his body strained. But it felt good. He felt alive.

Trapped...but alive.

3

"Training area. Five minutes. Then we're off like a herd of turtles."

At the sound of her father's voice, the corner of Neelu Otus's mouth curled up, forming the hint of a lopsided smile. She looked to the door of her room, where Eldrick stood, a black travel duffel bag slung over his shoulder. He tapped the watch on his wrist for emphasis and hiked up an eyebrow for added effect.

"Be there or be triangle?" she asked.

"You got it," he said, disappearing down the hall.

Neelu returned to her own travel bag and the tangle of clothes next to it. She crammed a red sweater into the bag, and topped it with her large electronic notepad and noise-canceling headphones.

There was little else in the world that she cherished as much as her relationship with her father. Their shorthand—comprised of humorous phrases he'd used when she was a little girl—always reminded Neelu of her childhood, of carefree days at the beach, of the sand in her toes, the sun on her shoulders, and the surfboard under her arm. This was before her mother died, of course. Before the constant running and fear of danger.

Before the Revolution.

Eldrick used the phrases less often now, but they still contained that little bit of magic in them, like the comforting warmth of a security blanket, and she could tell that he knew this. Her father was not made of stone, after all. He just acted that way around the others.

Neelu shouldered her bag, closed her door, and walked down the cement hall to the main training area. The unfinished, open space contained a small half-pipe and an array of angular cement ramps and metal rails and flatbars. They were all enclosed by a dirt BMX path. It was a smaller space than the sprawling facility the Revolution had used in Phoenix, more industrial with exposed rafters. It was cold and unwelcoming. Hopefully, their stay here would be temporary.

Neelu saw Omar skating on the course. He was crouched low on his board, the familiar blue crackle of his Fragment emanating from the deck's composite wheels and dancing around his skate shoes. He rode along the series of ramps as if he were a bird skirting light and effortless across the clouds. He ollied off a ramp, twisting in the air and landing perfectly atop the metal rail of another in a flawless lipslide.

She felt her pulse momentarily quicken as he smoothly transitioned into a new trick. Once, ages ago, she had kissed him. She'd given him CPR also, but that didn't count; his mouth had tasted like seawater and fish then. But the kiss was an impulsive decision. She didn't regret it, but they had also never mentioned it again.

A door slammed, and she saw her father striding across the training area from the secure equipment room. In his hands was a small, lead lockbox.

"Hey, Neelu." Omar's voice behind her startled her. A stray dreadlock fell across her nose, and she blew it out of her face.

"Oh. Hey," she responded, flustered.

"Are you ready?" her father asked as he approached the two.

Neelu nodded.

"Where are you going again?" Omar asked. He kicked his board up into his hands and slung it casually over his shoulders.

"San Francisco," Eldrick answered. "The meeting is between the Revolution founders. We'll be discussing not only how to retrieve the Fragments stolen by the Collective, but also the artifact you uncovered in Egypt." He held up the lockbox, then slid it safely into his bag.

Recently, the team's Phoenix facility had been compromised, and the Collective had stolen their cache of Fragments. After this, the team had found a piece from an ancient Egyptian shield, a powerful object known as a totem that was akin to the mystical 900 skateboard. The teens had gone after the piece alone, not knowing what it was they were even searching for at the time. Omar had stepped forward, taking command and leading a broken, untrustworthy team back to a cohesive unit.

"Rafe is also away on Revolution business," Eldrick said, referring to his second in command, a no-nonsense man who Neelu never really cared for. "So you four are on your own. Stay alert, work on your training, and we'll be back in two days."

"Yes sir." Omar popped off a quick salute, dropping his board to the cement with a loud clatter. "See you in a few, Neelu," he said as he kicked off and sped toward the nearest ramp.

"Later!" she shouted after him, watching him for a lingering moment as he lifted off the ramp and spun in a perfect 360. Then she followed her father, like she always did, toward the waiting Black Hawk helicopter.

FRAGMENT

POWER QUEST

ENTERED OMA

REVOLUTION VISIO

APOCALYPSE AM

K SKATE KESTRE

ENERGY DESTIN

4

Two days and four flights after his bizarre Parisian episode, Mikey stood outside a Seattle skatepark in the rain. He traced the outline of the cut on his neck with the tip of his index finger, and absentmindedly scratched at it. The park, located in a section of town called Fremont, was nothing too spectacular. Nearly every inch of the white brick building was sprayed with colorful designs or ornate signatures.

A dented, metal door on one of the graffiti-tagged walls banged open and two teens exited. They flipped up their hoods against the rain and dashed off toward a nearby convenience store.

Mikey crossed to the door, caught it before it swung shut, and slid inside. Wedged between his back and the pack on his shoulders was his board. He pulled the hood of his charcoal gray sweatshirt low and tried to remain inconspicuous.

He'd been to three other skateparks that day looking for Slider, or for someone who'd seen or recognized him. At the last place, a kid with multiple eyebrow piercings and a straight-billed Mariners baseball cap had said, "Yeah, the cocky Yankees dude? I've seen him kickin' over at the Works Skate Shop."

Mikey had barely made it through the door when he heard a voice call out, "That's the best you've got?!"

Standing on the coping of a battered half-pipe, the nose of his board jutting out into space and his arms open wide, was Slider. Mikey was hit with a rush of relief at seeing his foster brother alive and well. And from the sound of it, he hadn't changed a bit.

A group of teens huddled together near the pipe. Some held bottles of soda or energy drinks. A boy, around sixteen or so, stood on the opposite side of the pipe from Slider, waving off Slider's obnoxious taunt. The kid hitched his cargo shorts up and wiped his brow with the sleeve of his long flannel shirt.

"You think you can top that, bro?" the teen shouted at Slider. A wide smile spread across his face.

"Think? Nah," Slider said. "Know? Absolutely!"

Slider dropped into the pipe. He made a few passes, crouching down as he crossed the flat and raising himself on the upward slope to gain speed, a technique known as pumping. Mikey was amazed at how skilled Slider had become. After one last pass, Slider shot up the transition of the pipe and into the air. He executed a pitch-perfect 540 McTwist, landing backward on the pipe, riding up the other side, and dismounting directly next to the kid in the flannel shirt.

The crowd whooped and hollered, but Mikey noticed something odd about Slider's board. Though not vibrantly glowing, it appeared as if the tail of the deck was pulsing with a cool, blue light. It made him think about the artifact he'd deposited in the Skate-O-Rama locker back in New York. The one that had started this whole mess.

Was it possible that Slider still had it?

Mikey reached into the front pocket of his hoodie and withdrew the cell phone Venin had given him. He took a deep breath, exhaling slowly through his nostrils.

Now or never, Mikey thought.

Using his thumb, he punched in Slider's cell number from memory, then typed a text message: HEY BRO, IT'S MIKEY. IN SEATTLE. U THERE?

Mikey didn't take his eyes off his foster brother. He was afraid the teen might vanish in a cloud of smoke, like an illusion. The sound of a personal ring tone—a Jay-Z song—filtered from a bench beside the pipe. A blonde girl, obviously familiar with Slider's stuff, rummaged through a blue pack and pulled out a phone. She glanced at the screen.

"Dylan!" she shouted, her eyes not leaving the cell phone.

Slider was still trading comedic insults with the other skaters.

"Dylan!" she shouted again.

This time, she got his attention. "What's up, Ames?!" Slider saw the look on her face and quickly clambered down off the pipe. She didn't respond. Instead, she waited until he was close and handed over the phone.

Even from this distance, through the crowd and the dim lighting, Mikey could see the variety of expressions and emotions wrestle their way across Slider's face.

He swayed, looked like he was going to faint, and then sat heavily on the bench.

Mikey scratched at the cut on his neck. Then, he blended into the crowd and exited the skatepark, phone in hand, hoping Slider would text him back.

A half hour later, as Mikey skated down a wet sidewalk, dodging puddles the best he could, the phone in his hand buzzed. He braked under the blue awning of a supermarket and checked the message.

WHO R U? NOT A FUNNY JOKE, read the text from Slider.

Mikey responded: IT'S ME. DO U NEED ME 2 CATCH A JETER FOUL BALL 2 PROVE IT?

Once, when Mikey and Slider were in the foster system, Mikey had snagged a couple of seats to Yankee Stadium. He and Slider had cut out of the foster home without telling anyone and watched the Bronx Bombers pummel the White Sox. During the game, Mikey had used his soda cup to catch a foul ball hit by the Yankee shortstop, a memorable experience that left both boys covered in Coke and rolling in the aisles laughing. It was one of the best days of Mikey's life. Returning to the foster home that night, they'd been reamed a new one, but it had been totally worth it.

Mikey waited under the awning for another text. Down the street, a crowd of people shopped at an outdoor seafood market.

Buzz. MIKEY?! WHERE R U?!

SEASIDE FISH MARKET ON 34TH.

Buzz. BE THERE IN 10.

***

While he waited for Slider to show up, Mikey sat on the back bumper of a refrigerated truck in the heart of the market. He watched the men and women working at a variety of stands and booths. They shouted at one another, flinging enormous fish—salmon, swordfish, and others—through the air to one another, catching them in the folds of brown paper. It was an amazing, almost hypnotic sight.

Soon, Mikey heard the rattle of two skateboards weaving through the crowd. Slider appeared, an anxious, determined look on his face. His eyes scoured the mass of shoppers. Behind him was the girl from the skatepark.

Mikey hopped down off the truck and waved an arm in the air. Slider nearly fell off his board when he saw Mikey. He leaped off the deck while it was still moving, and enveloped him in a massive bear hug.

"Oh man, I thought you were dead," Slider's muffled voice said.

"Same here, dude," replied Mikey.

They held on for a long time, as if letting go meant losing one another again. Slider was the closest thing Mikey had to family, and it felt good to have him back.

Slider relented. He held Mikey at arm's length and gave him a once-over. "Where the heck have you been?"

Mikey shrugged. "Around."

"You've dropped, like, twenty pounds," said Slider.

"I've been hiding out. Those dudes that came after me…I didn't want them coming after you, you know?"

"Yeah, well…," Slider began, "I've got a lot to tell you about those guys."

Mikey's eyes drifted over Slider's shoulders, to the blonde. She was holding both skateboards now, having picked up Slider's abandoned deck.

Slider caught his glance. "Oh right," he said, pulling the girl toward him. "Mikey, this is Ames—I mean, Amy—Kestrel. Amy, this is my foster brother Mikey."

"Nice to meet you," Amy said. She had an incredulous look in her eyes, like Mikey was an urban legend come to life.

"Likewise," Mikey replied.

"What about Benny and Jeannine?" Slider asked.

Mikey shook his head. "Don't know," he said. "I stayed away. They'd been through enough, man. Wasn't going to put them in danger again."

"Did you try to talk to a cop named Case?" asked Slider. "Before he was killed, he was the detective in charge of tracking you down."

"I was going to see him," answered Mikey. "I even made it to the station, but I overheard someone saying he'd been found dead, and I panicked. Flew the coop before I talked to anyone."

"Well, I can't even tell you how awesome it is to see you again, bro," Slider said. "How'd you even know where I was?"

Mikey had anticipated this question, too, and had concocted a half-truth he hoped Slider would buy. "I hitched a ride west from a guy I knew in NYC. His band had a gig out here. Thought I should finally get out of town while I could. When I got here, I heard some kid ranting about you. Not a lot of cocky skaters in a Yankees cap named Slider, right?" Mikey struggled to keep eye contact with Slider as he lied.

"Wow, that's pretty convenient," Amy said.

"Yeah," he answered. "Guess I lucked out."

"I'll say!" Slider slapped Mikey on the back. "So where're you staying?"

"I was hoping I could crash with you," said Mikey.

"Oh." Slider was taken aback. Mikey hadn't expected his brother to balk at the suggestion, and he suddenly realized it might be harder to accomplish his task than he originally thought.

"Is that cool?" Mikey asked.

Slider thought it over. He looked at Amy, who stared at him apprehensively. Finally, he said, "I don't know, man."

"Seriously?" said Mikey.

"I'm sorry, bro," Slider replied. "I...can't let you."

"Wow. That's cold, dude."

"Hey, it's not like that. Know what, let's get a burger. I can fill you in on why you can't. It's a loooong story."

Mikey could feel the panic rising in his chest. "Come on, man. I just—"He'd almost blurted it out, almost told Slider everything. Then he remembered the audio chip in his neck, and wondered if Venin or one of his goons was listening in to their conversation. He scratched at the cut on his neck, furious that he was breaking Slider's trust, but afraid of losing his memory even more.

"Mikey, if you only knew what I've been through—" said Slider.

"What *you've* been through?!" Mikey dropped his board to the ground and stepped on. "You don't even know the half of it. Thanks a lot…bro." He spat out the last word like it was poisonous and would kill him if it lived in his system any longer.

"Mikey, wait…" Slider started.

"I'm outta here." Mikey kicked off and skated away, past stands filled with the thick, pungent scent of fish, crab, and shrimp.

Maybe it was better this way. Sure, he was peeved at his brother, but now Mikey didn't have to break Slider's trust. Yeah, he'd become a drooling, mindless zombie when Venin found out he'd failed and zapped the device in his neck. But if he never remembered his past, then he didn't know what he was missing, right?

In the distance, he heard Slider call out his name once, twice, and by the third time, it was barely loud enough to hear over the noise of the market.

Then, he heard Slider shout, "Okay! Fine! You can stay!"

Mikey stepped on the grip tape of his board, stopping abruptly.

He stayed that way for a moment, mustering up the courage to turn around. He was just starting to come to terms with the impending, horrific conclusion to his brief existence. But now, it seemed as if instead of losing his mind, he'd be losing the one thing more important in his life: his brother.

Mikey weighed his options as oblivious shoppers swarmed past him, neatly packaged fresh seafood under their arms. He wished he could be the bigger man, be the hero, stand tall and face the end like a fighter. But he was not. He was terrified. And because of that overwhelming fear, he turned around and skated back toward Slider and Amy.

5

Tommy spent most of the day trying to shake the memory of his father. He was annoyed at himself for even thinking about Henry Goff. The man had walked out on his family, had left his mother alone to raise and support a child. And his mom was never the same after his dad up and vanished. She always had that faraway look in her eyes, like she was imagining a better life somewhere. Like she regretted the one she had. Tommy hadn't thought of his dad in ages.

He was laying on the futon, staring at the pocked ceiling in the bunker. His hair, still damp from the shower, soaked into the thin pillowcase.

I've gotta get out of here, Tommy thought.

Tommy didn't know if it was intuition, or the lingering affect of the Fragment's powers, but he knew that Archard Venin was coming for him. From the first time they'd met, the Collective agent always had something up his tailored sleeve.

Tommy closed his eyes and let his mind wander…

***

…A wave crashed against his face, dousing fifteen-year-old Tommy with saltwater. His eyes stung. The taste in his mouth was nearly enough to make him gag. A strand of seaweed was plastered to his cheek.

"Stay alert, Tommy!" came the wisdom of Zeke Grebes, about five seconds too late.

Tommy wiped the seaweed and water away with the palm of his hand. He was standing waist deep in the Pacific Ocean, a vibrant red surfboard floating beside him. Omar, now a lanky twelve-year-old, sat straddling his board twenty feet further out into the surf. Beyond Omar, lying on his lucky surfboard and smiling back at them, was Omar's dad, Zeke. Tommy knew exactly what type of board the surf legend rode. Any chance he got, Zeke would rattle off its name with religious awe: "A 1965 Greg Noll Slot Bottom," he'd say. "Riding this killer is like shooting a curl on a little slice of Heaven."

The afternoon sun glinted off the water; its shifting reflection forced Tommy to squint in order to see Omar's dad on his turquoise board. Zeke waved one of his tanned, muscular arms. "Come on, boys! The next set of waves has your names written all over them."

Tommy reached for his surfboard. A spray of water, splashed up by Omar's hand, caught him in the face.

Omar laughed. "You heard the man, ya barney," he said, mimicking his father. "Let's surf!"

Tommy slid onto his board. He paddled hard with both arms, feeling the burn. But he was cool with the pain. Being out here on the water with Zeke and Omar, he was finally starting to feel normal again.

After his father left, Tommy's mother spiraled into a depression. He would find her at all hours of the day sitting on the couch, watching television, the bowl of cereal he'd left her with hours earlier half-eaten and abandoned on the cushion beside her.

Zeke had noticed the neglect, and had taken Tommy under his wing. He'd always treated Tommy like he was special. Now, it felt like he was Zeke's second son.

"Who wants the first one?" Zeke asked.

Omar didn't even hesitate. "On it!" He began to furiously paddle before the next swell passed them.

Omar leaped to his feet, surfed across the crest of the breaking wave, then down its face. Zeke laughed, a hearty sound that carried over the water. It was a laugh that made Tommy's heart burst with admiration.

Zeke placed a hand on Tommy's shoulder. "You're next, son," he said. "You'll do great. Just stay radical!"

"Yes, sir!" Tommy craned his neck to watch behind him, so he could time the wave. As it approached, he paddled furiously in the same direction. He felt the wave lift and carry him on its back. He quickly popped up onto his bare feet, steadying himself. When he had his balance, he sliced down the smooth surface of the wave. He was cautious, though. Zeke Grebes' first rule of surfing: "Respect the ocean, and it'll respect you."

Tommy crouched, let his hand glide across the crystal surface of the wave, and stayed up. Tommy moved in a huge arc, bringing the nose of his surfboard around and pointing it in the air. It was a move Omar had taught him. It wasn't pretty, but he nailed it.

When the wave flattened, Tommy glided toward the shoreline. He heard a whistle, and saw Omar standing in the sand waiting. "Nice roundhouse, bro! Learn a few more moves like that, and you can sign up for the next Junior Oceanside Surf Championships."

"Yeah, right," Tommy scoffed. "You could totally do it. Win one of those monstrous trophies like Dad's."

"Your dad is the best surfer I've ever seen." The boys looked back at the ocean, where the legendary Zeke Grebes soared off the lip of a wave, like a bird taking flight. Around him, the setting sun left the sky and clouds a beautiful combination of purple and pink.

Before long, the trio of surfers rode their last wave and drove back along Seacoast Drive. After they pulled into the Grebes' driveway and got out, Tommy hiked up his backpack and climbed on his skateboard. His house was only three blocks away.

"Are you sure you don't want to join us for dinner?" Zeke asked. "Rachel's making crab legs."

Tommy shook his head. "Nah, I'm sure Ma's whipping up something semi-edible. Thanks, though."

Tommy rode home by cover of streetlights, a cool breeze kicking off the ocean and giving his bones a chill. He rounded the corner onto Beech Street, dodged the McPherson's sprinkler as it arced out into the sidewalk, rattled up his driveway, kicked his board up into his hands, and burst inside.

"Ma?!" he shouted. "I'm home!"

No answer.

Suddenly, he heard gunshots from the living room. He instinctively ducked, before noticing the flicker of the television screen against the walls of the dark room, and realizing the gunfire was from a TV program. He peered in. Sure enough, his mom was asleep on the couch, oblivious to the loud noise filling the house.

Tommy descended the stairs to his room, saw a sliver of light coming from the door. He entered, and as he closed the door behind him, a voice from the corner said, "Lovely day for surfing, eh?"

Startled, Tommy spun to face the intruder. A man in his fifties, give or take, stood near the desk. He was looking at a poster of Kelly Slater on Tommy's wall.

"Who the heck are you?" Tommy asked. The man's presence in his room annoyed him, but for some reason, it didn't outright scare him.

The man offered his hand. "Archard Venin," he said.

Tommy didn't move. "Get out of my house."

Venin dropped his hand. "If you'll just give me a moment, Thomas," he began, "I'd very much like to discuss your father…and your destiny."

"Pops walked right out the door and never looked back." Tommy held his skateboard like a baseball bat, ready to swing. "I suggest you do the same."

"Henry Goff is a good man. Zeke Grebes on the other hand…" Venin let the statement dangle.

Tommy snatched it up. "What about Zeke?"

"Zeke Grebes is not the man you think he is. He's not a friend, and he's certainly not your father." Venin walked toward Tommy. He held out his hand again. This time, he held a business card between two fingers. "Here," he said.

Tommy thought for a moment, and then seized the card without looking at it.

"When you want to know the truth, Thomas, you let me know," said Venin. He strode past Tommy and without another word, or even a look back, he opened the bedroom door and was gone…

***

…Tommy didn't know it then, but Archard Venin changed his life that night. He'd saved Tommy from living in Omar Grebes' shadow, and taught him the truth about Zeke, the man he'd treated like a father.

Tommy climbed out of the futon and stretched.

It was only a matter of time before Venin would save his life again. All he had to do was be patient.

Just a little while longer.

FRAGMENT
POWER QUEST
ENTERED OMA
REVOLUTION VISIO
APOCALYPSE AM
SKATE KESTRE
ENERGY DESTIN

6

"Welcome to the Revolution, Mikey."

Mikey, in a clean, dry set of clothes, was walking around the Revolution warehouse on the outskirts of town. Slider was giving him a tour of the place. As they meandered through the training area, Mikey spied a secure door with a digital keypad next to it. He'd been told to look for a locked room, that he'd most likely find the information about Tommy there.

As they walked, Slider filled Mikey in on the Revolution's mission to retrieve the Fragments of Tony Hawk's 900 skateboard. It was a lot of information to wrap his brain around, but Mikey was starting to see how the puzzle pieces fit together.

The tour ended in a sprawling kitchen filled with industrial-sized steel appliances. The rest of the gang were seated at a table and eating two fresh, large pizzas.

Slider hooked his board on one of the metal chairs. Mikey nodded in its direction. "So that Fragment on the deck...that's part of Tony Hawk's board from the X-Games?"

Slider balanced a drooping slice of supreme on his fingers, pulling off a hunk of melted cheese. "Yep," he replied. "One of the few we have left."

"And that's what I had back in New York?" asked Mikey.

"Yeah," Slider answered. "It's why the Collective attacked you."

"And all four of you have them?"

The dark-haired kid named Omar piped up. "They're the only ones we have left," he said. He lifted his own board up and spun one of the wheels. It crackled with weird blue electricity.

"Watch out!" Mikey tried to warn Omar before the deck electrocuted him.

"No, dude. It's cool." To illustrate his point, Omar held his hand near the wheel. The cobalt glow sparked around his splayed fingers but didn't burn his flesh.

Joey dug a necklace out from beneath his shirt and displayed his Fragment. Amy, still looking uncertain, didn't offer her Fragment for show and tell.

Slider passed Mikey a slice of pizza and jumped up to sit on the metal counter top. "So here's the deal: you can stay, but only for one night."

Mikey nodded. "That's cool."

"We've had problems in the past with security breaches, but I told these guys it wouldn't be a problem, cuz you're my bro. Right?" He smiled and clapped Mikey on the shoulder.

"Right," Mikey answered, a little too quickly. The false sentiment sounded hollow to him, and he swallowed hard.

What if I say, Screw it, and don't go through with it? Mikey thought. *I can still back out, can't I? Tell Slider everything? Warn him about Venin?*

Mikey scratched at his neck, more intensely than ever before.

"You okay, man?" Omar asked.

"Yeah, I'm fine," Mikey answered.

"I hope so," Slider said, "cuz we're about to find you a board and hit the ramps." Snatching one more slice for the road, Slider led Mikey toward the training area.

7

"Well, it ain't the Hilton, but it'll have to do." Slider tossed two thin pillows and a blanket at Mikey.

They were in Slider's room, exhausted after a night of popping ollies and grinding flatbars. It had been a long time since Mikey had ridden like that, and he was beat. Slider, on the other hand, looked like he hadn't even broken a sweat. He claimed it was the Fragment, that it boosted his energy and skills. Mikey had tried to use Slider's board, but the Fragment didn't have the same effect for him as it did for his brother. Further proof that Mikey's role in this whole mess wasn't as significant as Slider's.

"Dude, last month I was sleeping in the back of a Volvo," Mikey said. "A warm blanket and a hard floor sound like five-star digs to me."

"Good, because there's no maid service," said Slider. "And I don't leave a mint on your pillow."

"Fair enough," Mikey replied.

"Oh. Got something for you." Slider rummaged through his nightstand, snagging an item from the clutter and holding it out to Mikey. "I was hoping I'd be able to get it back to you someday."

In his open palm was a small leather band. Attached to it was a silver watch face.

"Wow," Mikey said, astonished. He'd lost the timepiece during his scuffle with the Collective, when that dude Rodney had clocked him so hard, he'd fallen to the ground and split his lip open on the curb.

"Glad it's back in the right hands, bro," Slider said, his voice breaking just a bit.

"Thanks."

They settled in for the night. Slider clicked off the desk lamp, plunging the room into total darkness. It took a few minutes for Mikey's eyes to adjust, but soon, he could see the faintest outline of the door, and the sliver of light seeping in from under it.

Mikey lay on the cement floor for what felt like
hours, though was probably only a matter of minutes.
He was wired, and wanted nothing more than for
the whole thing to be done. To get out of here in the
morning, and hope that Slider was none the wiser.

Wishful thinking.

Finally, he could hear Slider's breathing slow in a
deep, steady rhythm, proof that he was asleep. Mikey
lifted the blanket off his chest and slowly stood up.
There was a soft click as he turned the doorknob, and
the door swung open soundlessly. He waited until he
was sure Slider was still snoring into his pillow, then
slithered out of the room.

The hall was lit by a series of small, emergency
bulbs along the ceiling. They cast the space in an odd,
purple light. He headed left toward a 'T' in the hall,
passing the other teens' bedrooms.

The training area was dark. Mikey used a flashlight
app on his smartphone to guide him to the secure room.
He eyed the keypad adjacent to the doorframe.

One of Venin's goons, a tech-savvy girl named
Sophie, had run through the steps he would need to
crack the password. First, he needed to attach the phone
to the keypad using a small, black cable.

Check.

Then, open the program, hit Search, and let the phone work its magic.

He did, holding his breath as four boxes lit up on the screen. Each had their own shuffling set of numbers, like an alarm clock gone berserk, as the program tried to crack the password. One by one, the numbers lit up. When all four were displayed on the phone, Mikey held his breath and punched in the four-digit code.

The deadbolt disengaged.

He was in.

Mikey stepped into the room, leaving the door cracked behind him. Using the smartphone's flashlight, he found a small floor lamp and clicked it on.

The dim light left the room half in shadows. Rows of skateboard parts—trucks, axles, and small crates of wheels—filled metal shelves. There were even empty skate decks, signed by pros like the Bones Brigade, Elliot Sloan, even a Ryan Sheckler original, hanging along one wall like an art display. A half-dozen surfboards, including a classic turquoise blue longboard, were stacked in one corner.

On the other side of the room was a slew of high-tech electronic gadgets.

In the center of the room sat a glass display case. It held nothing but air now, but he imagined this was where the team had kept Fragments of the 900 board.

No time for gawking. Have to get a move on, be all snug as a bug again by the time Slider wakes up.

There was a metal desk cluttered with books about Egyptian history, scraps of paper filled with notes, and a flat-screen monitor pushed back against the wall. Two computer towers sat on the floor beside the desk.

"Bingo."

Mikey was still a bit of a newbie when it came to computer stuff, so it took him a minute to fumble around for a way to boot up the computers. Once they were both quietly humming, he tried to recall what Sophie had told him about the next step.

"Open the secondary program," she'd said, "and if the device is anywhere within a five-foot radius of the computer, it should start backing up the files."

Mikey set the phone on the desk, pressed the appropriate icon, and waited. An empty bar popped up on the phone's screen, along with the words: 0% DOWNLOAD COMPLETE.

The bar suddenly began to fill and turn green, and the number began to steadily rise.

Mikey sighed deeply in relief. Just another minute or two, and he'd be in the—

"What are you doing?"

Mikey's blood ran cold at the sound of Slider's voice. He slowly turned. Blocking the doorway, arms crossed at his chest, was Slider. Behind him were the other three Revolution members.

None of them looked happy. The pained, hurt expression on Slider's face, though, was nearly too much to handle.

"Hey…" Mikey started. Behind his back, the phone continued to download the computer's contents.

"I asked you a question," Slider said, barely containing the rage swelling up inside him. "What. Are. You. Doing?"

"Would you believe looking for the bathroom?" Mikey tried to joke.

Slider rushed forward. He clawed at Mikey's shirt, grabbed the collar, and shoved him back against the desk. "This isn't a joke, man. I trusted you! What are you, a Collective snitch now?"

"Wait!" Mikey pointed at his neck. "I had to. They put something in me. If I didn't do what they said, they'd erase my memory. Everything just…Gone."

"Who did?" Amy asked from the doorway.

"I...I can't tell you," Mikey replied.

"The Collective?" Omar asked.

Mikey shook his head. "No, they're listening. They could fry my brain any second, if I tell you too much. Heck, they might do it anyway." He squeezed his eyes shut, wondered if he would feel the zap, or if he'd just...change.

Behind him, the smartphone chirped. The download was complete.

"What was that?" Slider asked. He released Mikey, shoved him aside, and searched for the source.

"I'm so sorry, bro," Mikey said quietly. "I hope one day you can forgive me."

Mikey grabbed the nearest board, the Sheckler, off the wall. Catching the team off-guard, and using the deck like a shield, he barreled past Omar and Amy. He knocked Joey clean to the floor as he pushed his way out of the equipment room.

Some of the florescent bulbs on the ceiling were now faintly glowing. It wasn't a lot of light, but it was enough for Mikey to see where he was going. He hopped on the board and kicked off across the training area.

"Stop him!" Omar shouted, followed by the sound of running footsteps. Mikey rode through the array of angular ramps, heelflipping off and front Smith grinding across a low rail. He dismounted onto the top of another ramp.

Out of the corner of his eye, he caught a cobalt flash. It was Omar, riding hot on his Fragment-enhanced board.

"Mikey!" Omar shouted, "I just want to talk! What were you looking for?!" He hit the top of a ramp and kickflipped off.

"Just let me go!" Mikey shouted back.

Without answering, Mikey swerved in Omar's direction. He narrowly avoided colliding with the teen. Omar was forced to brake hard. He tumbled from his board, landing on the hollow ramp with a thud and rolling safely away.

Ahead of him, on the far cement wall, Mikey saw the small steel emergency exit. He rode up the last ramp and shot high into the air. He sailed over the dirt BMX track, noticing midair that Joey was pedaling furiously along the path in his direction. He landed cleanly about five feet from the door, stopped, and scooped up the board.

He drove his shoulder into the steel exit. It slammed open, and he rushed out into the cool Seattle night.

The deck's wheels rattled over the cracked, wet cement of the warehouse's expansive lot. Mikey reached the chain-link fence surrounding the property. He heaved the board in a wide arc over the fence, then climbed as fast as he could. The metal dug into his fingertips, tore at his skin. He didn't care.

When his feet hit solid ground on the other side, he hazarded a glance at the building. The door was wide open, and he could see Omar and Joey scampering out.

Mikey's vision blurred.

It's happening, he thought. Then he realized his impairment was not caused by the device, but rather by tears. He was crying. He used his hoodie sleeve to wipe his eyes. He saw the leather watch on his wrist, a keepsake from a life he could never return to.

Then he hopped on the stolen deck and pushed off into the dark night.

He was on his own again.

And if Venin didn't trigger the device in his head, he'd have to live with the betrayed look he saw in Slider's eyes for the rest of his life.

It was almost enough to welcome oblivion.

8

Ding! After staring at it for what felt like hours, the electronic notepad resting on the plane seat beside Elliot Addison finally chimed.

About time, Elliot thought, picking up the device. On the screen, a map of the United States was overlaid with a grid. As he watched, the grid shifted until a red dot appeared on the West Coast. Northern California, to be exact.

So this is where they're keeping Goff, he thought. *Good. We're close.*

"Is that from Venin?" The soft, silky voice came from across the row, where Lora sat with her legs curled under her on the plush, accommodating seat.

"Yes," Elliot answered. "Seems like our boy Singer actually came through."

"Good," Buzzer piped up. He was seated behind Elliot and sipping on a can of Coke. "I'm starting to get airsick. Another hour, and I would've needed this." He held up a thin, white paper bag.

The group—consisting of Elliot, Buzzer, Lora, and Sophie—had been flying in a private Collective jet for most of the night. It was now after midnight. But Venin had wanted them prepped and ready to swoop in when he finally had Tommy's coordinates.

"Get ready, team," Elliot addressed them. "Rescue mission is a go."

He felt the plane shift as it banked. The pilot must have received the new destination as well. The team stood, gathering their things and beginning to outfit themselves in black clothing, black elbow and knee pads, and Kevlar vests.

"You know," Buzzer joked as he strapped on a kneepad, "we need some kind of name."

"Our team has a name," Elliot said matter-of-factly. "We are the Collective, a cohesive agency with a singular mission. It would do you well to remember that."

"Uh, yes, sir," Buzzer grumbled. He silently returned to the business of preparation.

The phone in Elliot's pocket vibrated.

It was Venin.

"I'm to assume you've been redirected?" the Collective leader asked.

"Yes, sir," Elliot responded. "Target's location has been acquired, and we're en route. Looks like we're headed toward..." He checked the coordinates on the notepad. "...a coastal town named Arcata."

"Nothing fancy, Elliot," Venin said. "Just get in, get Tommy, and get out of there. Understand?"

"Roger that. What about Singer? Are you going to tell him that the GPS device you put in him can't really zap his memory?"

Venin chuckled. "No, I think I'll keep that to myself. Michael Singer could very well be a valuable pawn to have on our side of the board," he said. "Good luck, Elliot."

"Thank you, sir."

Elliot clicked off his phone and picked up the black parachute pack resting on the floor by his seat.

Time to go to work.

***

Neelu could hardly keep her eyes open. She'd been quietly sitting in the conference room for most of the night, listening as the twelve Revolution founders—men and women from around the globe—droned on about the Collective, about the missing Fragments, and about the Egyptian artifact. Her eyelids felt like lead. She needed a jolt of caffeine, and wished she had a grande mochachino on the table in front of her.

She snuck a glance at her phone to check the time. It was 12:30 in the morning. Way past her bedtime.

Just then, the phone began to belt out the opening chords of a Pink song, startling her so much she nearly dropped it. A dorky photo of Omar making a face and sticking out his tongue popped up on the screen.

Neelu silenced the phone. Too late. Everybody in the room was now staring at her.

"Sorry," she said.

"Everything all right, Neelu?" her dad asked.

"Dunno. I'll check." Embarrassed, she stood and skulked out of the room.

She answered the phone in the hallway. "Omar, why are you calling so late? Is something wrong?"

Omar's answer was a static-filled jumble. She was going to have to go outside.

"Hold on, I can't hear you," she said. She spied the abandoned office complex's emergency stairs nearby and quickly took them three at a time, bursting out into the cool San Francisco night. She walked along the edge of a small pavilion in front of the building.

"Okay," she said, slightly winded. "Hit me."

"Neelu, we screwed up," he blurted out.

"What happened?" she asked.

Neelu listened, horrified, as he filled her in on the details of the night. By the time he'd reached the part where Mikey stole a board and hightailed it from the facility, she had chewed her fingernails down to nubs.

"This is insane. How am I going to tell Dad?" She posed the question more to herself than to Omar.

"I'm sorry…" said Omar.

"There's a room with the founders of the Revolution in it, people I'm about to seriously upset," said Neelu. "'Sorry' doesn't cut it."

Neelu disconnected the call before he could respond. *Probably for the best*, she thought. *I may have said something I'd regret later.* It upset her, though, that sometimes Omar could still be so childish.

She composed herself, took a few relaxing breaths, and climbed the steps back to the conference room.

Neelu's father could tell something was amiss right away.

"What's happened?" he asked.

"The Collective," she said. "They've…infiltrated the Seattle facility."

"What?" Her father was beside himself.

"Is the team all right?" a mocha-skinned woman named Yasmin asked.

Neelu nodded. "They used Dylan's foster brother, Mikey," she replied. "He was caught downloading files off Dad's hard drive."

"What were they after, Eldrick?" a British man named Arthur asked, his thick jowls pursed into a grimace.

Her dad thought for a moment, then said, "It's Venin. He's coming for Tommy Goff."

"Are you sure?" Daniel Solomon, a man wearing a suit far too big for him, asked. As he spoke, he nervously fidgeted with the handle to his leather briefcase.

"I'm positive," Eldrick answered. "The safe house has been compromised. We're going to have to move him. I just hope it's not too late."

Eldrick swiftly picked up his satellite phone and began to make arrangements.

The room was again abuzz with activity. And Neelu, her pulse racing, wanted nothing more than to go back in time fifteen minutes, when the world hadn't gone topsy-turvy, and when the only thing on her mind was a blast of chocolatey caffeine.

9

Tommy was awakened from a light sleep by commotion upstairs. It wasn't much, just a raised voice or two and the sound of shuffling steps, but this late at night any noise was suspicious. He rolled over and glanced at the glowing blue numbers on the alarm clock beside the futon.

1 A.M.

A knowing smile danced on his lips. He was fully awake now. Rolling out of bed, Tommy pulled a faded red sweatshirt over his head and jammed his feet into his skate shoes.

Venin had finally sent the team for him...

***

…Tommy rolled down the transition of the empty pool and landed hard on his right shoulder at the bottom. His board skittered away as he groaned and raised himself up to his knees.

"You all right, Tommy?" Omar asked from his perch atop the wooden half-pipe. The two had spent the afternoon hanging at the skatepark attached to Billy's Board Shop, one of Tommy's new favorite haunts.

Tommy wiped his hands on his shorts and adjusted his helmet, which had twisted in the fall. "Yeah. Nothin' bruised but my ego. And my head."

"You've been crashing and bailing all day, dude," said Omar. "You sure you're okay?"

"Yeah. I'm fine." He wasn't, though. The stand-up frontside 5-0 he was just performing on the pool's coping should have been routine. He'd done the move a million times. But Tommy hadn't been able to nail a trick all day, and he knew why.

Archard Venin.

It'd been a week since he'd entered his bedroom to find the French dude waiting for him, spouting his nonsense about Zeke.

Shouldn't trust him? Tommy thought. *Zeke's the only person I can trust…right?*

Tommy kicked his board in frustration. It clattered away, up the transition, and back toward him.

In one smooth move, he stomped on the deck's tail. It popped up into the air. Tommy caught it and walked to a patched blue booth with exposed stuffing and springs. He sat heavily.

After a couple of minutes, Omar slid into the booth across from him. "You know you're going to have to tell me, right?" he said.

Tommy scratched at a curse word etched into the table between them. "It's nothing, man." The truth? He really did want to tell Omar, but for some reason thought it was foolish. And potentially dangerous. He didn't want to bring Omar into this if he didn't have to.

"Wanna blow this popsicle stand?" Omar asked.

"Yeah."

The duo blasted into the hot San Diego afternoon, skating their way through a small commercial district and taking a shortcut through a junkyard and back to their neighborhood.

They reached Omar's house just as Zeke's wagon was pulling out of the driveway. Brake lights blazed as the two teens rode up beside him. Tommy noticed the Slot Bottom strapped to the top of the car.

Zeke hung his head out the driver's window. "Aloha!"

"Hey, Dad!" said Omar. "Hitting the waves?"

"Not tonight," Zeke replied. "Just getting ready for tomorrow. Going to sneak in some waves before we celebrate. Say, are you coming to the birthday breakfast feast in the morning, Tommy?"

Tomorrow was Omar's thirteenth birthday.

"Well, it's kind of a family thing," Tommy said.

"Hence the invite, son." Zeke winked at him, then threw up his fingers in a peace sign. "See you in the morning, Tommy!"

"You bet," Tommy answered with a smile.

Zeke began to drive away, hollering out the window, "Stay radical, boys!"

Omar shook his head as his dad drove away. Then he and Tommy bumped fists. "Later."

"Later, bro." Omar jogged across the lawn to his welcoming house and his loving family—one that Tommy was happy to be a part of.

He stood in the quiet street and watched as Zeke's taillights shrank toward the horizon. *That's it*, he thought, *time to give Archard Venin a piece of my mind.*

As he pushed off and began to skate home, he pulled out his phone and punched in the number.

It rang three times. "Thomas," Venin said calmly, "I've been waiting for you."

"Listen, dude," Tommy said, crouching low and turning south down Palm Street. "Leave me alone. Zeke Grebes is a good man. He—"

"Not on the phone, Thomas," Venin interrupted him. "I have something I'd like to share with you."

"What?" asked Tommy.

"The Imperial Beach Pier. I assume you know of it?"

"Yeah. So?" replied Tommy.

"I will be there in fifteen minutes," Venin said. "And I would appreciate it if you would meet me there."

Tommy opened his mouth to tell the man off, but before he could, he heard the click of Venin hanging up.

Furious, Tommy ollied high into the air and onto the sidewalk. Then, he changed directions and headed back toward the ocean.

***

Imperial Beach Pier at sunset was a busy place. Lovebirds strolled hand in hand along the shore. Fishermen dropped their lines off the end of the pier, hoping to snag a big one. Cutting across the waves, glowing in the fading light of the magic hour, were a number of surfers.

Tommy's board clattered across the wooden planks of the pier. He ignored the disapproving looks he got from passersby. He was on a mission.

There.

Standing near a food cart in a suit that made him stick out like a sore thumb was Venin. In his hand was a black attaché case. Tommy skidded to a stop in front of him.

"Beautiful evening, isn't it, Thomas?" Venin asked, ignoring Tommy's impatient expression.

"Seriously?" Tommy hissed through clenched teeth. "Dude, I can't believe you made me come all the way out here to tell you off."

"Yes, yes," Venin said, dismissing Tommy with a wave. "I'm sure you have a noble speech all planned out in which you defend the honor of Zeke Grebe. I'll save us both some time, as it's getting dark." He placed the attaché case on a bench and gestured for him to sit. "Humor me."

"No. Just…just leave me alone." Tommy turned and began to walk away.

"He doesn't love you."

The four words stung more than Tommy thought they would. He stopped cold.

Tommy shouldn't believe this guy, and he sure didn't trust him. But there was that little part of him, the insecure part that wondered why his father left, that was curious.

"How do you know?" Tommy asked.

"Because even though he treats you like a son, Zeke Grebes is not your family," said Venin.

"What makes you so certain, Mr. Know-It-All?" asked Tommy.

Venin nodded in the direction of the case. "Listen for yourself."

Tommy sat on the bench. Venin removed a pair of earbuds from the case and handed them to the teen before depressing a button on the device they were attached to. As Tommy inserted the earbuds, he heard a static crackle, followed by the sound of a conversation.

"Zeke, how are you?" the first voice asked.

"Copacetic," answered the familiar voice of Zeke Grebes. Tommy felt uncomfortable listening to the conversation, like an unwelcome guest at a party.

"And how is our young daredevil?"

"Goff?" Tommy's heartbeat quickened at the sound of last name. Zeke laughed. "The truth? He scares the crap out of me, Eldrick."

"You can understand why Henry left then, eh?"

"The kid's like a time bomb," said Zeke. "I just hope I'm nowhere near him when he decides to blow up."

"You know what they say: 'Keep your friends close and your enemies closer,'" Eldrick said.

"And how long will I be 'keeping him closer?'"

What? What is Zeke talking about? Tommy was baffled. *Was Zeke really talking about him?*

"Until the Revolution founders are sure he won't fulfill his destiny. Does that bother you?" asked Eldrick.

Zeke sighed. "No. I just…he and Omar are so close. I don't want Tommy around my son any longer than I have to. Is that clear?"

"Crystal," Eldrick replied.

The line crackled back to static as the two men hung up. The betrayal Tommy felt in his heart was unbearable. He'd loved Zeke Grebes, had thought of him like a father. But now? Now it was as if one more person in his life had turned their back on him. Like he was a poison that was rotting everyone around him to nothing.

Tommy ripped the earbuds out and tossed them aside. Venin patiently waited, hands in pockets, for Tommy to speak.

"So what is my destiny?" Tommy finally asked.

A wide smile spread across Venin's face. "I thought you'd never ask," he said.

And like that, Tommy's true purpose had changed…

***

…Of course, he'd only meant to ride in on the jet ski and scare Zeke Grebes, send a message that Tommy was no longer playing by the same rules. He never intended to kill the man. But it's not like Venin cared; he'd clapped Tommy on the back and praised him for his actions.

The door to the basement slammed open with a thunderous, resounding *BANG!* Two men in dark clothes entered the room. Tranquilizer guns were holstered on their belts.

"Where are we going, boys?" Tommy asked.

Without a response, the men used zip ties to cuff Tommy's hands behind his back and led him out of the bunker for the first time in months.

10

Elliot Addison guided his parachute into a small, moonlit clearing. He landed heavily. The shock vibrated up his legs and snatched the breath from his lungs. He didn't have time to be in pain, though. Before the others landed, he quickly bundled up the black canvas chute and stowed it under a nearby shrub.

Sophie swung down next, landing as gracefully as a cat. Lora touched down fifty feet to the south, near the edge of the clearing. Buzzer came down hard on his backside, so as not to re-injure his ankle sprain from the failed mission in Egypt.

The team assembled on the west side of the clearing, where Elliot crouched.

The screen of his GPS-tracking watch reflected off their black helmets and bathed their faces in red light.

"Target is two hundred yards west." Elliot pointed through the towering redwood trees surrounding them. "Stay low and follow me."

He led the way into the woods, weaving between the massive trunks and exposed roots of the majestic redwoods. The team made little sound as they moved.

Before long, they heard voices. The sound of an idling engine. A door slamming closed. *This isn't part of the plan*, Elliot thought. He climbed a small rise, crouched low to the ground, and saw a small rambler-style home nestled in the trees. A black van was parked in front; its rear doors were open. Beside the van were two motorcycles.

The front door of the home swung wide, and two men in dark clothing led a figure in red out to the waiting vehicle.

"Where are they taking Tommy?" Buzzer whispered from beside Elliot.

Elliot turned to face the others. "Someone's called an audible. We go to Plan B."

Buzzer lumbered up from his stooped position and removed a Fragment from his pack. "You ready, Lora?"

"Always," she replied.

Buzzer and Lora held their Fragments in front of them. The shards began to twitch with red electricity. The air burned crimson as the artifacts transformed into sleek, black skateboards.

"That never gets old," Buzzer said with a chuckle.

"Stay in contact with your earpieces, and stay by the road," Elliot explained. "Sophie and I will be along shortly."

"Copy that." Buzzer hefted the skateboard under his arm. Then he and Lora took off through the redwoods.

***

The first Revolution guard, a wiry, muscular man with a tattoo of a flaming skull on his neck, shoved Tommy roughly into the back of the van. There were no seats, just a plywood floor. Tommy's face mashed into the gritty board and he struggled to right himself. One of the other guards was already behind the wheel of the van, while a third rode shotgun.

"Let's haul tail, Richards," Tattoo Guy said. He slammed the doors shut, then banged on them twice with his open palm. "Once Burton is off the phone with Otus, we'll catch up to you on the PCH."

The Pacific Coast Highway? So we are still in Cali.

Richards, an overweight guy in his late thirties, put the van in gear and accelerated away from the house.

The ride was brutal, as Tommy had no way of supporting his weight. With every turn or bounce, he ricocheted around the van like a human pinball. From what he could see out of the windshield, it looked like the van was driving along a winding, cliffside road. Tommy could see the ocean to his right, far below them, cast in the moon's shimmering glow.

"What the—?" Richards hollered. He slammed on the brakes, and the van came to a screeching halt. Tommy fell forward, smacking his shoulder and face hard on the plywood.

"What are you doin', Richards?!" the passenger asked. "Just go!"

Tommy struggled to rise, looked over the driver to the windshield, and saw two figures bathed in the headlight's glare. Buzzer stood with a smile on his hulking face, a skateboard slung over his shoulder. Next to him, holding her board at her side, was Tommy's beautiful girlfriend Lora, looking stunning, as usual.

As Tommy watched, Buzzer's skateboard pulsed with red energy. Tendrils of lightning cascaded down his arm.

"Give us Goff, and we'll let you live!" Buzzer shouted.

A panic-stricken Richards turned to face Tommy.

Tommy shrugged. "Looks like the cavalry's here, boys," he said.

***

Neelu sat in the corner of the conference room, her legs up on the chair and her arms hugging them tightly, watching as her father took command. She was truly in awe of him. His poise, his coolness under pressure. He had been on the phone for a half hour, instructing the men at the safe house on where to relocate Tommy Goff, while around him, the other Revolution founders fumed over the breach in security.

Eldrick disconnected. "Alpha team is moving Tommy now," he said. "Bravo team has cleared out of the safe house and is following suit."

Neelu couldn't stop thinking of Omar, about how she had hung up on him, how angry she'd been. Not because he didn't deserve it; she wasn't worried about hurting his feelings. No, she felt bad because she had not let him explain the full story. And no one had spoken to the team since that initial, abbreviated conversation.

As Eldrick continued to relay information to the room, remaining calm and collected as always, Neelu stood, snatched her skateboard off the floor, and snuck into the hall. She was going to give Omar a ring. Besides, it's not like anyone would notice her absence. And she could use a little fresh air anyway.

Down the emergency steps, slower this time, and out into the crisp early morning. Her breath plumed in front of her.

Neelu crossed the pavilion and sat on a short brick wall, away from the building. As she picked up her phone, though, she noticed a black sports car idling down the street, its headlights off.

Suddenly, the side door of the building banged open, startling Neelu. She ducked back into the shadow of the adjacent building, watching as someone ran across the empty pavilion.

It was David Solomon, the nervous Revolution founder with the briefcase.

Wait…where's his briefcase?

Neelu opened her mouth to call out to Solomon, who was making a beeline for the sports car, then thought better. A deep, overwhelming premonition suddenly hit her like a freight train.

"Dad," Neelu hissed. She turned, began to bolt back across the pavilion when—

BOOM!!

The building erupted in a giant ball of flame!

The shockwave lifted Neelu off her feet, sent her soaring backward. The earth shook. The pavement buckled. She landed hard on her back, and the wind was knocked out of her. The heat was so intense, it stung her eyes and seared her face. Flames licked high into the air, and the smoke and fire seemed to scorch the starless sky.

She stumbled to her feet, shocked into silence. It was gone, all of it. The building, the Revolution...they were gone. He was gone.

Her father was dead.

Neelu knew she should run. She should get away from the fire and smoke and swirling ashes, but her feet were like roots burrowed deep into the cement. She was planted in her spot. The depth of loss she felt was only just scratching the surface. If she let it consume her now, she'd never get out alive.

Behind Neelu, on the street, the engine of the black sports car revved. In all the chaos, she had forgotten about David Solomon. *He did this*, she thought, fleeing.

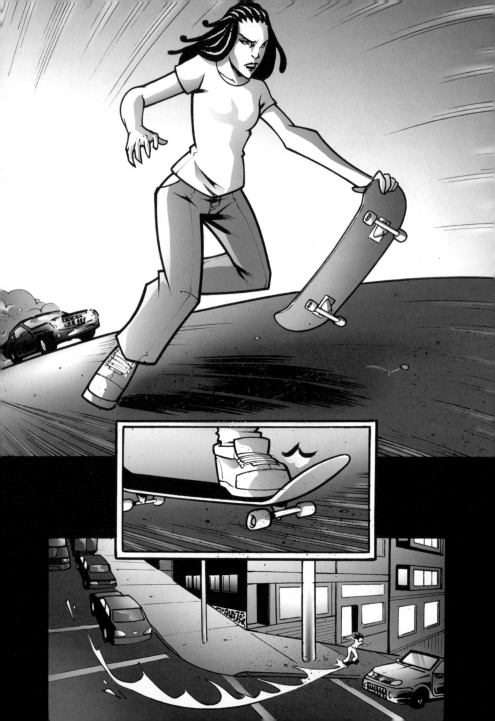

11

The skateboard beneath Buzzer's feet radiated with a deep scarlet energy as he barreled down the winding Pacific Coast Highway. Elliot, leaning forward on the sleek motorcycle, watched as the hulking teen skated down the hill after the van holding Tommy. Because of the hairpin turns and narrow ditches along this portion of the highway, the van was forced to remain at a manageable speed, thus enabling the skateboarding teens to somewhat keep pace.

Elliot breezed past a sign indicating the highway curved left.

"Buzzer. Lora. Watch it. Turn coming up," he warned the others via headset.

"Got it, Boss-man," Buzzer answered.

Easier said than done, though. As Buzzer began to lean into the sharp left turn, his board slipped on him. He began to career toward the cliff, and the steep, treacherous drop to the ocean below. The only thing between the teen and an unscheduled flight was a battered metal guardrail.

The floundering Buzzer had one choice: he ollied into the air, twisting his body as he soared toward the cliff. He hit the guardrail perfectly, locking his rear truck in a backside grind. White and red sparks lit up the road like fireworks beneath his deck. He rode the rail as it curved left, his back facing the sharp, sudden drop to the ocean. He dismounted safely back onto the road before the rail disappeared into a small copse of roadside shrubs.

"Sick move, Buzzer!" Sophie said over the earpiece.

"Thanks! It was nothing!" he joked.

The van had gained distance on them. Elliot spied Lora a few feet to his right and motioned to her. "Lora! Latch on!"

She nodded, leaned left, and grabbed onto the motorcycle's metal seat frame. Elliot twisted his wrist, gunned the bike, and they rocketed forward.

"You okay?" he asked her as they swerved left to avoid Buzzer, then back before an oncoming car splattered them like a bug on its windshield. It blared its horn at the motorcycle.

"Yeah!" she answered.

Elliot looked at the van and saw the flat stretch of road in the distance ahead of it.

"We need to act fast," he told her.

"Then get me out in front of it, and give me enough room. Time for some drastic measures."

"Got it. Hold on tight!"

He gunned it, and they cruised up alongside the van. Elliot caught the bewildered expression on the driver's face as they shot like a bullet past the vehicle. Lora's board was smoking. The red electricity was keeping it steady, but the wheels were spinning faster than ever.

Lora let go of the motorcycle, stooped low for less resistance, and raced to the bottom of the hill.

"This is gonna hurt," Elliot heard her mutter, just before she shoved the tail of her deck into the asphalt. The board split; wood splintered up into the air behind her. She twisted on her board, slowing herself further by executing a desperate manual.

"One shot is all you're going to get," Elliot said.

Sophie—with Buzzer clinging to the back of her ride—was close behind. "Make it count."

The moment she came to a stop, Lora kicked the deck up into her hands. The van was barreling toward her. Tendrils of energy erupted from the board as it shifted and changed in her hand. The slivers of wood littering the PCH shot into the air and reattached to the deck as it transformed and shrank.

When it was back in Fragment form, Lora snatched the artifact and pointed it at the van. The driver must have seen her, because he slammed on the brakes.

A blast of red electricity burst from the Fragment in her hand. It connected with the front left tire of the van. The rubber popped and sizzled as the tire melted.

The driver tried to retain control of the van, but it was clear that the van now had a mind of its own. The vehicle cut left, then lifted onto two wheels. It crashed hard onto its passenger side. But it did not stop.

"Lora! Get out of the way!" Elliot shouted as he watched the van skid down the hill toward her. Lora did not move, just stood her ground and watched.

The crumpled, smoking van came to rest just five feet from where Lora stood. Elliot revved the engine of the motorcycle and rode back to the crash site.

"Pretty sure this isn't the rescue mission Venin had in mind," Elliot said as he removed his helmet.

Lora crouched down and looked through the windshield. The two guards were dazed and coughing, hanging sideways by the shoulder straps of their seatbelts, but otherwise not seriously injured.

There was a banging sound coming from the back. Lora walked through puddles of leaking radiator fluid and oil to the van's rear. She pried open the double doors, which protested with a loud groan.

"Nice night for a drive, eh?" Tommy staggered from the van, his hands bound together with zip ties. His face had a healthy collection of scrapes and bruises. He doubled over and coughed.

"You okay?" Elliot asked, removing a utility knife from his cargo pants and using its blade to slice the ties on Tommy's wrists.

"Never better," Tommy said. "Let's get out of here."

While it hadn't gone according to any plan Elliot could have conceived, they had Tommy. Venin would be upset, but Elliot was going to call this one a win and leave it at that.

Together again, the Collective team disappeared down the moonlit Pacific Coast Highway.

12

Neelu rode the trolley to the bottom of Hyde Street and then walked to the bayside area of San Francisco known as Fisherman's Wharf without running into the sports car. There was traffic here, as well as insomniacs and night owls meandering down the sidewalks even at this late hour.

She stopped near a well-lit newsstand to catch her breath. Her side ached, her legs felt like rubber. She leaned against the stand's wooden magazine rack, then slid to a sitting position.

"Hey," said the stand owner, a thickset man with a baseball cap pulled so low his ears jutted out at a funny angle, "You okay, kid?"

Neelu used her dirty arm to wipe the soot and sweat from her face. "No," she said, "I'm pretty far from okay."

"You need help? Like a cop or something?" He was genuinely concerned.

She shook her head. She couldn't trust anyone, except... *Omar*, she thought.

Neelu pulled her phone from her pocket. She needed to call Omar, needed to let them know what was happening. That her father was...

Just then, Neelu felt the overwhelming grief bubbling to the surface, pressing against her resolve.

And then she saw the sports car.

It was rounding a corner not fifty feet from her. She quickly rose, watching as the driver came to stop.

They'd seen her.

"I really think we ought to call the cops, kid," the stand owner reiterated, but Neelu barely heard the man. She was already sprinting away from the newsstand, across the sidewalk and toward the bay. Behind her, the car revved its engine and continued to pursue her around the next corner, onto another street lined with brick buildings. Bass-thumping music suddenly filled the air, and Neelu saw salvation ahead.

A dance club.

A crowd of people milled about outside the club. Many wore glowing necklaces or swung them in the air. Neon lights flooded the crowd with brilliant hues of purple and green.

Neelu ran into the crowd, threaded her way through the mass of sweaty, gyrating patrons. She was swallowed up by them, and when she tried to peer through the maze of bodies, she could no longer see the sports car.

Need to find a safe place to call Omar.

The building that housed the nightclub was a four-story brick structure, and Neelu was certain she'd find a fire escape in the adjacent alley. She slid around the corner unseen. Sure enough, a rickety metal staircase led to the building's roof. She quickly pulled herself up, scrambling up the fire escape to the building's flat, tar-covered roof.

She had a beautiful, bird's-eye view of the city that, under different circumstances, would have amazed her beyond words. The San Francisco Bay stretched out before her. She could see the Golden Gate Bridge to her left, the island of Alcatraz straight ahead.

Neelu pushed the beauty aside and dialed Omar's phone. He picked up on the first ring.

"Neelu, hey," he said. "Look, I want to—"

"They're dead," she blurted out, interrupting him.

"What?" asked Omar, puzzled.

"The building…it's gone. They…they blew it up. Everyone's gone, Omar." And with that, she broke down. Omar patiently let her. He didn't press her, didn't ask questions; he was just there, his breath on the other end of the line, waiting for her to continue.

And in that moment, she knew why she cared for him. His patience. And his heart.

Finally, when the tears ran dry, Neelu spoke again. "They had an agent," she said. "One of the founders. He must have planted something in the building. I was outside when it went off."

"Are you sure they're dead?" Omar asked in disbelief.

"Yes."

Though he tried desperately to mask the fear in his voice, Neelu could hear it. "We're not safe here. We'll have to take whatever money we have, whatever equipment we can, and just leave."

"What about Rafe?" If there was any silver lining to this terribly dark cloud, it was the fact that Warren Rafe was out there somewhere, safe. Hopefully.

"He'll find us. I'll make sure of it."

"And where will we go?" she asked.

He thought for a moment. "Do you remember where we met?"

How could she forget? Dragging him from the ocean, lifeless, and performing CPR until he coughed up water and called her an angel. "Yeah."

"There," she said. "In two days. The four of us will be waiting for you."

She was about to hang up when Omar said, "Neelu?"

"Yeah," she whispered back.

"You're the strongest person I know," he said. "Don't give up hope. Find me, and we'll figure this out together."

"Thanks."

Neelu hung up. In the distance, she heard the sound of sirens. Turning away from the bay, looking back into the city, she saw the pillar of smoke still rising into the night sky. All it took was a moment, an instant, the tiniest fragment of time, and life could change. All her hopes and dreams, the memories to be made with her father…they were all gone now. Gone in a blink.

In that one instant, the Revolution as they knew it had been altered forever.

ABOUT TONY HAWK

TONY HAWK is the most famous and influential skateboarder of all time. In the 1980s and 1990s, he was instrumental in skateboarding's transformation from fringe pursuit to respected sport. After retiring from competitions in 2000, Tony continues to skate demos and tour all over the world.

He is the founder, President, and CEO of Tony Hawk Inc., which he continues to develop and grow. He is also the founder of the Tony Hawk Foundation, which works to create skateparks and empower youth in low income communities.

ABOUT THE AUTHOR_

BRANDON TERRELL is a Saint Paul-based writer and filmmaker. He has worked on television commercials and independent feature films for almost a decade. He has also written dozens of comic books and children's books. When not writing, Brandon enjoys watching movies, reading, baseball, and spending time with his wife Jen and their son Alex.

AUTHOR Q & A_

Q: WHEN DID YOU DECIDE TO BECOME A WRITER?

A: I've been writing and telling stories all of my life. I still have notebooks filled with childhood mysteries I wrote that were inspired by The Hardy Boys and Encyclopedia Brown. I love the idea of engaging a reader by finding an unexpected way to tell a story. It's been a lifelong passion of mine.

Q: DESCRIBE YOUR APPROACH TO THE TONY HAWK'S 900 REVOLUTION SERIES.

A: My approach always starts with the characters, and trying to find new and exciting ways for them to showcase their extreme talents, while still telling a story that packs an emotional punch. Then I try to imagine locations that are visually interesting as well, places where the Revolution team will be out of their element. While I'm not a globe-trotting traveler myself, some of the locations I've written about are places I've visited at one time or another. What's fascinating about the series is that it blends multiple genres (mystery, action, science fiction, romance, etc.) all in one book, so the story possibilities are endless!

TONY HAWK'S
900 revolution

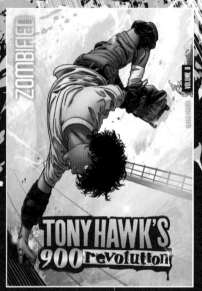

TONY HAWK'S 900 REVOLUTION, VOL. 9: ZOMBIFIED

Once more beset by visions, Omar finds himself trapped inside one. The world he sees is vastly different than the one he left. In this postapocalyptic vision, the Collective has defeated the Revolution. In their absence, the disbanded Revolution has been replaced by a group of tribes that skate in their honor. Omar searches for his friends, for the meaning behind this horrific vision, and for a way out!

TONY HAWK'S 900 REVOLUTION VOL. 10: UNEARTHED

Omar convinces Eldrick Otus to him lead the Revolution on a t to recover a Fragment in Egy When they discover the Fragme is resting deep within a forgott pyramid, Omar sends Joey a Amy after it. The Collective, led Elliot Addison, causes the pyramic entrance to collapse. The tee must work together to retrieve t Fragment and find a way out, befc

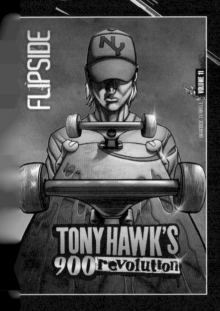

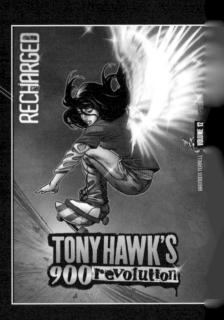

TONY HAWK'S 900 REVOLUTION, VOL. 11: FLIPSIDE

The Collective, in possession of the Fragmented board and growing stronger every day, decides to retrieve one of their own: Tommy Goff, held captive by the Revolution in an undisclosed location. To discover the prisoner's whereabouts, Elliot Addison and his mentor Archard Venin must earn the Revolution's trust. But Archard has other plans — the destruction of the Revolution, and the death of his old friend, Eldrick Otus.

TONY HAWK'S 900 REVOLUTION, VOL. 12: RECHARGED

Omar Grebes and the team me Fiona Skylark. Shrapnel from childhood accident is embedded the girl's stomach. One of the piec is from the 900 board, makir Fiona a walking, talking Fragmer The team must keep her safe fro the Collective. The biggest shock yet to come, though, when Om comes face to face with a ve much alive Zeke Grebes, who invit them to join 'The New Revolutio

RECHARGED

Omar Grebes stared up at the expanse of blue sky and watched a single cloud drift lazily toward the sun. He rested on his surfboard, floating in the ocean and letting the ebb and flow of the Pacific move him. Closing his eyes, Omar felt the sun's warmth radiate off his skin and absorb into his orange rash guard. His feet dangled off the sides of the board and into the water. He swirled them back and forth.

This is as close to perfect as it gets. I wish I could freeze this moment, live in it forever...

"Hey kid! You aren't giving up on me, are you?!"

Omar propped himself up and yelled back, "Give me a break, Dad! We've been out here all afternoon!"

"The day's not over yet! No time for relaxation!"

From his position further out in the frothy waves, where he sat straddling his turquoise surfboard, Zeke Grebes smiled at his son. Deep creases formed on his tan face, weathered by years of exposure to the sun and saltwater, two elements that flowed through his veins and energized him more than guzzling a pot of coffee.

Wait. Something isn't right…

"So the question is: are you gonna stay put?" Zeke asked. "Or stay radical?!" Then he slid onto his stomach and began paddling out toward the horizon.

What's going on? I thought Dad was…

Ahead of Omar, a bird suddenly dove from the sky and pierced the surface of the ocean. Then another. Another. Omar noted the birds' brown and black plumage. They were grebes, a stunning waterfowl, and Omar's namesake. Like heavy raindrops, the flock of grebes splashed into the ocean around him. They swooped across the sky in patterns too numerous to count. It was almost like…a dream.

In the blink of an eye, they were gone. Not a single bird remained in the sky or on the surface of the ocean. Confused, Omar paddled out to meet his father.

"What took you so long?" Zeke joked. "Feels like I've been waiting forever."

Omar missed days like this. It had been an eternity —two years, when Zeke was caught in a wave and disappeared into the ocean—since he'd surfed with his father.

A large swell approached, rolling forward like a freight train. "This one is all yours, son," Zeke said.

Omar turned to face the shore, pumped his arms and propelled forward. The wave churned beneath him, lifted him like a bird taking flight. He stood, gripped the fiberglass board with his toes for balance.

It feels so real. The waves. The board beneath me…

Omar carved down the wave's face. He arced back and forth until the lip of the wave crested behind him and curled into a massive barrel. He was too far ahead of the tube, so he stalled by applying pressure to his back foot and driving his hand into the wave until the barrel cascaded over his head and enveloped him.

Omar plunged underwater, twisting and spinning in the undercurrent like he was stuck in the rinse cycle of a washing machine. The Velcro from the ankle leash ripped free. He didn't know which direction was up or down, and when he opened his eyes, all he saw was swirling darkness. His hands grasped for silt, sand, coral. Anything. The pressure in his chest was intense. His lungs burned.

From nowhere, Omar felt a hand grip his wrist, and he was pulled upward until he broke the surface of the water. Omar took deep, greedy gulps of fresh air. He opened his eyes and noticed the sun had disappeared behind a thick layer of gray, imposing clouds.

His father was gone, but Omar was not alone. Neelu bobbed in the water beside him.

"Why am I always saving you?" she asked before swimming in a front crawl toward the beach.

Omar followed. As he stood in the shallow water and trudged toward shore, lightning crackled through the sky. It was not typical lightning, though; the bolts of electricity illuminating the darkness were a deep crimson. *Okay…time to wake up…*

Omar saw dozens of surfboards lining the sandy shore. They were stuck into the ground and pointed toward the stormy sky. The sight was disconcerting. It looked as if he were walking through a cemetery, that each board was a gravestone marking someone's eternal resting place.

Sure enough, the first board he approached was a recognizable turquoise blue, a '65 Geg Noll Slot Bottom with a name etched into its wood-grain stripe: ZEKE GREBES.

Omar ran his fingers over the inscribed name.

"I'm sorry, Dad."

To his right, he noticed another board. This one bore the name ELDRICK OTUS.

Read more in the next adventure of…

Tony Hawk's 900 Revolution

TONY HAWK'S
900 revolution